This book belongs to

MIKI
....

Address
....

Age
....

Written by Anne McKie. Illustrated by Ken McKie.

Published by
Grandreams Limited
435-437 Edgware Road, Little Venice, London, W2 1TH.

Printed in Hong Kong.

TEDDY
On Safari

Teddy was puzzled, he told his friends so.
"What's going on? Does anyone know?
There's a secret for sure, and I've got to find out,
What all the mystery and whispering's about!"

Just then the 'phone rang.
"It's a long distance call.
     Hurry up!" cried Mother,
       "and come to the hall.
It's your uncle from Africa -
Game Warden Bear,
       He wants all you young bears
       to visit him there!"

The next week the bears
were so busy all day,
   Getting passports
   and tickets to go far away.

"Let's sit on each suitcase," Teddy said with a grin
   "It's a bit of a squash getting everything in!"

They checked-in at the airport, and then said goodbye.
Their plane looked so big, could it really fly?

They took-off from the runway - the trip had begun.
"Hurrah!" cheered the bears. "This will be fun."

The flight was so long, it took almost a day,
But the bears knew that Africa was a very long way.

When at last the plane landed, all four Teddies ran,
    To meet Uncle Bear, in his Game Warden's Van.
"You'll be tired," he beamed, "after such a long ride."
    "Not a bit!" yelled the bears, as they clambered inside.

The airport and buildings were soon left behind.
On through grasslands the road seemed to wind.
"Was that a giraffe?" the bears squealed in delight.
"Look zebras!" laughed uncle. "Let's give them a fright!"

Uncle's Game Warden Van was striped black and white,
It was painted that way to keep out of sight.
"We'll get close to the animals, as close as we dare,
You must keep very quiet, and take great care."

Uncle told the four friends, "We should head for home.
The sun sinks so fast here, it's no place to roam!"
As darkness fell, strange sounds they heard.
Was that noise a lion, or simply a bird?

Uncle said with a grin, "You'll be safe as can be,
  In my Game Warden's Lodge, high up in this tree."
Very soon the Teddies were tucked up for the night,
  Dreaming of adventures to come, when it's light.

At first light of day, what a hullabaloo,
　　Hyenas, zebras and pink flamingoes.
Each morning they came for a drink at sunrise,
　　Right next to the tree-house. What a surprise!

The Teddies crept out on the platform to see,
　　Elephants and lions, as close as can be.
"This water hole's famous," said uncle with pride.
　　"Sit here and watch, I"ll bring breakfast outside!"

"It's still very early, the day's just begun,
    You must dress in light clothes, and wear hats in the sun."
How uncle laughed, when at last they were ready.
    "Here's a badge for you all, that says Game Warden Teddy."

Next they heard uncle calling, "Be as quick as you can.
Stop what you're doing and run for the van.
There's a fierce-looking rhino heading this way.
He seems rather angry. I don't think we'll stay!"

The bears hung on tight, as the van drove off fast.

"Oh, no!" gasped Teddy, "he's seen us drive past!"

Uncle shouted, "I'm going as fast as I can."

But the rhino was faster and caught up with the van.

SMASH! went his horn into the van's side.
The Teddies looked round for somewhere to hide.

Uncle jammed on the brakes and the van stood quite still,
But the rhino charged on and ran over the hill.

"Wow, that was close!" uncle said with a smile.
"I'll turn the van round, he'll be back in a while!"
So they crossed a wide river, left the rhino behind,
But swimming towards them - what did they find?

"Crocodiles!" Teddy yelled, then turned to see,
A large herd of hippos that looked so friendly.
Uncle parked on the bank, "It's quite safe to get out.
The young ones will come if you give them a shout."

Baby hippos came out of the water to play,
"This is sure to be fun," Teddy cried, "can we stay?"
They dived in the river, then splashed mud around,
Rode on the big hippos, but were quite safe and sound.

Too soon it was time to wave new friends goodbye,
And drive back in the van to their tree-house so high.
Safe in bed they would dream of adventures to come,
And tales they would tell, when at last they flew home.

TEDDY
and The Robot

Early one morning, just before eight,
As Teddy was sitting on top of the gate.
He spied the mail-van parked down the lane,
"Poor Post Bear has broken down again!"

So they loaded the parcels onto a small truck,
    Which Teddy had found in his tool shed. What luck!

"I'll fetch you some help,"
Teddy called, "if you wait.
I'll call all my friends -
so the mail won't be late!"

"There's lots to be done," smiled Postman Bear.
"I've only three bags! Can two of you share?"

The bears took the letters and parcels to town,
    To houses and shops, every street up and down.
They worked hard all morning, each bear did their best,
    'Til the mail-bags were empty - just one parcel left.

The address on the top said,
'Professor T. Bear'.
  On one side a label read,
  'Handle with care'.
The professor answered the door with a smile,
  "This parcel's for Robert! Come in for a while!"

"Go into my study, there's room for four,"
    And as they sat down, Robert came through the door.
The Teddies just sat there, then gasped with delight,
    At Robert the Robot, so shiny and bright.

"Let's play!" clattered Robert,
- giving Teddy a squeeze.
    "Robert!" the professor smiled,
    "you must say please!"

In Robert's parcel were
games of all sorts,
    Bats, balls and racquets
    for every sport.
But Robert the Robot
didn't know how to play,
    So he tried them together,
    and all the wrong way.
The Teddies played cricket,
golf and baseball.
    "Games are lovely," cried Robert,
    "let's play them all!"

Soon the Teddies were tired,
they fell flat on the ground,
So Robert whizzed off
and brought their truck round.

"Hop in and I'll tow you home in a flash!"
"Oh, dear!" gasped Teddy. "I hope we don't crash!"

obert sped like a rocket down the long lane.
  They climbed up the hill, then flew down again.

It's like hanging onto a ride at the fair!"
  Gasped Teddy, (who'd rather be home in his chair).

Then Robert saw Post Bear still parked in the lane,
"Don't worry, I'll get your van started again!"
"Well done!" cried Post Bear and drove off with glee.
"I'll finish my rounds, then take you to tea."

So Robert went home with Teddy and friends.
  "I have a machine I would like you to mend."

"My garden's untidy!" sighed Father Bear.
  The lawnmower's broken beyond repair."

Now before Father Bear
could walk down the path,
Robert mended the mower
then cut all the grass.

He snipped the hedge, hoed the borders - not one
weed in sight,
Then he hung out the washing, Mrs Bear got
a fright.

At last Post Bear came back, "Hurry up!" he called.
    "Jump in my van, there's room for you all.
I'll drive you down to the park as a treat,
    And we'll see if Robert likes ice-cream to eat!"

"Has Robert been to a park before?"
    Asked the Post Bear as he opened the door.
But Robert had already rushed inside,
    And tried out the see-saw, the swings and the slide.

"Come on!" yelled Robert, "you're missing the fun.
Let's climb up the slide and go down one by one."
Then suddenly all of them heard a strange cry,
And a runaway pushchair went hurtling by.

"Baby Bear is heading towards the lake.
If we don't stop his pram, it will be too late!"
The Teddies all ran as fast as they could,
"We're not quick enough," Teddy cried, "it's no good!"

All of a sudden
something flashed past,
    Only Robert the Robot
    could travel that fast.

He zoomed towards the lake at the speed of a jet,
    And grabbed Baby Bear - who was not even wet.

"What a hero!" sighed Baby Bear's mother with pride,
But Robert was back on the top of the slide.
"I've made so many new friends today,
But best of all, I've learned how to play!"

TEDDY
and The Fire Brigade

One morning in the autumn when leaves start to fall,
Teddy was outside his house, kicking a ball.
"I've nothing special to do," he sighed.
"I can't think of a thing, and I've really tried."

"Can you gather some logs for me?" asked Mrs Bear.
'Then I'll light a fire, there's a chill in the air!"
"Right away!" called Teddy and kicked his ball high.
'There's a pile near the shed that I know are quite dry.

"May my friends come to lunch?" Teddy asked with a smile.
"If I give them a call, they'll be round in a while."
"I'll cook sausages and beans!" laughed Mrs Bear.
"That's what they ask for each time they come here."

Mrs Bear struck a match to make the logs light,
But the thick clouds of smoke gave her a fright.
"Our chimney must be on fire! Help!" Teddy cried.
"Leave the room. Close the door. We must both
wait outside!"

"Send for the fire brigade, I'll make the call,"
        Just inside the back door was a 'phone on the wall.
Smoke poured from the house and swirled around,
        Teddy hugged Mrs Bear, "We're both safe and sound."

Just then Teddy's friends rushed out of the wood.
    "We smelled smoke and got here as quick as we could!"
Suddenly the fire engine came flying past,
    "Hurrah!" Teddy cheered, "you got here fast."

Leading Fireman Bear was the one to decide,
That masks must be worn to venture inside.
The smoke was so thick it was quite hard to see.
"There's no fire here, it's a real mystery!
We've found plenty of smoke, but no fire at all.
Did you see any flames when you gave us a call?"

"I've just had an idea!" said Fireman Bear.
  "Let's get down the ladders and see what's up there!"
He climbed to the top of the chimney so tall,
  And what did he find - but Teddy's football.

Grinning, he slid down the ladder with speed.

"Who was it," he winked, "did this terrible deed?"

"It was me!" said Teddy hanging his head,

As he shuffled his feet and went terribly red.

"Never mind," said mother, "there's no harm done.
　　We'll clear up the mess, then have lunch in the sun."
The fire crew stayed and helped put things right,
　　And everyone worked up a huge appetite.

It was just like a party, the bears had such fun.
        But Teddy felt sorry for what he had done.
"Cheer up," laughed the fire crew. "Climb up inside.
        Come and visit the station - we'll give you a ride!"
Teddy's frowns turned to smiles when the journey began.
        "Do you think, for today, I could be a fireman?"

At the station the fire chief shouted "Hello!
  Come and look round, there's a lot you should know.
When you join the fire crew you wear special suits,
  Blue tunic with belt and a helmet and boots."

How smart all four looked in their fireman's clothes.
  Said Teddy, "Let's help them and unroll the hose."

Now the fire crew were testing equipment that day,
   And all the Teddies just happened to be in the way.
The engine pumped water out in a jet,
   Straight onto the Teddies - who got rather wet!

Teddy then asked the fire crew, "What do you do
To reach the top storey on a rescue?"
"We've no problem at all, to reach we're quite able
With our longest ladder. It's called a turntable!"

Said the fire chief, "We're having a practise today,
   We would like volunteers to help right away,
To climb to the top of the building and shout,
   So the crews can take part in a full scale turn out!"

All the Teddies agreed
they could come to no harm.
And off went the fire chief
to sound the alarm.
CLANG went the bell,
the crews rushed to the fire,
The turntable ladder
went higher and higher.

"Help, help!" yelled the Teddies. "Save us, please do!"
  "Hang on!" Fireman Bear called. "I've almost
  reached you."
He grabbed hold of Teddy and held him so tight.
  "Be careful, don't drop me!" gasped Teddy in fright.

But Teddy was carried down
quite safe and sound.
What a relief it was
when he reached the ground.
Back up the ladder
went the fire bear, so brave,
There were three more Teddies
he still had to save.

When he carried them down everyone gave three cheers
    For the fire crew and the four brave volunteers.

Back in the station the crew took a break,
    While waiting for fires - they often had cake!

"When you want to go home, we will give you a ride.
    If you want to save time, down the pole you must slide.
For a real fire bear it's the only way,
    And you four have been proper Fire Bears today!"

TEDDY
on Television

It was raining and Teddy was stuck in the house.
Father Bear sighed, "Be as quiet as a mouse,
I have so many letters to write today,
Wish hard and the rainclouds may blow away!"

But all day long rain poured from the sky.
It was hard to keep quiet, Teddy really did try.
First he dropped all his books then fell over his chair.
"I can't work in all this noise!" frowned Father Bear.

So he picked up his paper and sat down to read.
   "Oh great," cried Teddy, "you're just what I need.
I'll do magic tricks for you. Just take a card,
   Then I'll make it vanish - if I try hard!"

"Not now," groaned Father Bear. "Some other time!"
But up on his knee Teddy started to climb.
"I'll show you my magic, right here in your chair!"
"Will this take very long?" asked Father Bear.

As Teddy began Father Bear gave a cry,
  He picked up his paper, "Just look what I spy!
A new TV studio quite close by here,
  Is open to visitors one day a year.

Tomorrow's the day.
Would you like to go?
  First you look round,
  then take part in the show!"
"That's brilliant," cried Teddy.
"I know what I'll do,
  I'll ask my three friends
  to come along too!"

So next day found the Teddies all ready to go
In a taxi, to visit the new studio.

When they arrived Teddy said, "Let's make sure,
We don't miss a thing!" So they tried the first door.

The Teddies were told to sit still in a chair.
  Someone powdered their noses and then brushed
  their fur.
"It's the make-up room," Teddy said, giggly with glee.
  "We must look our best to star on TV!"

The next door they came to said MAIN STUDIO.
"Quiet please!" yelled a voice. So they walked on tip toe.
There were cameras and floodlights all over the place,
And microphones dangled in front of your face.

The control room was next on their studio tour.
What a shock the bears got when they peeped
through the door.
A camera had filmed them wherever they'd been,
And there they all were on the monitor screen.

An interview next with a bear of great fame.

But not one of them could remember his name!

"Would one of you like to take part in a show?

A quiz game perhaps - to find out what you know!"

Now Teddy stepped forward, said he'd like to try.

    The others stepped back, because they felt shy.

"I'm quite good at card tricks," said Teddy with pride.

    "We've found a magician!" the Interview Bear cried.

Said Teddy "I'll do all the tricks that I know."

    "Great!" said the Interview Bear, "You've got your own show."

The Director told Teddy
just what he should do.
  He showed him the camera
  and let him look through.
Then Teddy met his assistant
who'd help with the show,
  She'd a sparkling costume
  with a blue sash and a bow!

At last the Producer called, "Time to begin."
   "Ready when you are!" Teddy said with a grin.
"I'd like to welcome you all today,
   To my own TV show," viewers heard Teddy say.

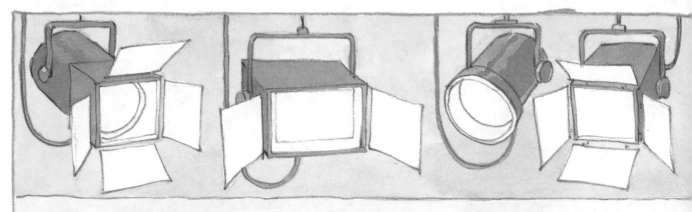

"Here is a card trick, you will not believe.
        My paws are quite empty and so is my sleeve.
Viewers at home, keep your eyes on this card."
        Then the studio audience clapped very hard,
As Teddy produced things out of thin air.
        Rabbits and flowers - even doves by the pair.

"For my next trick, my assistant, you'll see
　　Will step into this box - then I'll turn the key.
I shall count very slowly from one up to ten.
　　She'll vanish - then I'll bring her back again!"

Teddy opened the box with a turn of the key,
 Out jumped the Teddies - one, two and three.
"How that happened, I really don't know!
 Goodnight," Teddy bowed. "That's the end of my show!"

Mother and Father Bear could hardly wait
    For the taxi to bring the bears home to their gate.
When Teddy came in as tired as could be,
    Mother smiled, "We've been watching you on our TV"
But Father said, "Son I shall try very hard,
    To listen next time when you say PICK A CARD!"